E.T.™ THE EXTRA-TERRESTRIAL

Movie Storybook

adapted by Kim Ostrow
based on a motion-picture screenplay by Melissa Mathison

Simon Spotlight
New York London Toronto Sydney Singapore

A spaceship mysteriously landed in the middle of the forest, underneath an inky black sky. Strange creatures, no taller than children, waddled out, picked some plants, and brought them back to their ship.

One creature stayed behind to look at the trees. Out of nowhere several men started chasing the creature. Scared, he ran toward his ship, but it had already taken off. The creature's name was E.T., and he was now stranded on Earth.

"Can I play now?" Elliott asked his older brother, Michael. He sat at the kitchen table while his brother and his friends played a card game.

"Nope! But you *can* go wait for the pizza," Michael answered, making all his friends laugh.

Elliott grabbed his baseball and glove and ran outside. When he passed the toolshed, he heard a rustling sound.

"Harvey!" he called to his dog. But Harvey didn't come. Elliott decided to throw his baseball into the shed. To his surprise the ball came hurtling back and landed at his feet.

Elliott ran back to his house.

"Help! Let me in!" he yelled, banging on his back door. "There's something out there," he said, trying to catch his breath as Mary, his mother, opened the door.

"Who? The bogeyman? A goblin?" Michael said, laughing.

"I'm telling you," said Elliott carefully, "nobody go out there. . . ."

"Let's go!" shouted Michael, and he and his friends bolted out the door. Elliott and Mary followed.

"Something's out there," warned Elliott. "Look in the shed."

"I think the coyote's been back, Mom," said Michael, pointing to some strange footsteps.

"Okay, that's it," said Mary. "Party's over. Everyone back inside."

"There *was* something out there," Elliott told his mother as they walked back.

"I know, sweetheart," she said, ruffling his hair.

That night Elliott awoke when he heard a crash in the backyard. Grabbing his flashlight, he ran outside in his pajamas. He heard a croaking sound and walked through the tall cornstalks in the garden. It sounded like a frog. Elliott shined his flashlight toward the noise and came face to face with two huge eyes! Elliott screamed, and the creature screamed back. Petrified, the creature ran right past Elliott and out through the back gate.

"Don't go," Elliott called out, but E.T. was gone.

The next morning Elliott decided to ride his bike into the forest. Holding a full bag of candy, he searched the area.

"Hello!" called Elliott, dropping the candies and making a trail to his house.

Elliott waited in the backyard all day and into the night. He finally fell asleep in a chair, until a noise woke him up. When he opened his eyes he saw E.T. standing in front of him.

"Mom . . . Michael . . ." Elliott tried to speak, but barely any sound came out.

Just then E.T. shuffled closer to him. Elliott held his breath. Then E.T. extended his long skinny arm, opened his little fist, and dropped a handful of candy on Elliott's lap. Elliott smiled.

Elliott wanted to bring E.T. inside, so he made a new trail of candy leading to his room. "C'mon," Elliott called to E.T., who slowly followed Elliott, shoving candy into his mouth with each step.

Finally in the quiet of Elliott's room, they stared at each other. Then Elliott rubbed his nose. E.T. rubbed his nose too. So Elliott touched his mouth to see if E.T. would copy him. He did. Soon it grew late and both their eyes drooped sleepily. That night Elliott fell asleep while a creature from outer space watched over him.

The next morning Elliott faked sick and stayed home from school. When his mother left, he hopped out of bed and brought E.T. out of hiding.

"Do you talk?" asked Elliott. "Me human. Elliott. Ell-ee-ut. You extra-terrestrial. E.T."

But E.T. was too busy looking at everything in Elliott's room. "This is your home," Elliott showed him the nest he made for him in the closet. "Stay, okay? I'll be right here."

"How you feeling, faker?" Michael said to Elliott when he got home.

"Remember the goblin?" Elliott asked. Michael just laughed at him. "I'm serious. Can you swear to make the most excellent promise you can make?" Elliott asked.

"Okay," said Michael, "but you're pushing it."

"Close your eyes," Elliott said, bringing E.T. out of the closet. "Now turn around."

Just then Gertie, their little sister, burst through the door. She screamed when she saw E.T., and E.T. screamed back. Suddenly everyone was yelling at once.

After they calmed down, Elliott heard his mom come home. He pulled everyone into the closet and they all sat on the floor quietly staring at E.T.

"He won't hurt you, Gertie," Elliott said. "But you can't tell anyone about him."

"Why not?" she asked, clutching her doll.

Elliott thought for a moment. "Because grown-ups can't see him. Now, everyone promise you won't tell." And they did.

"We'll be right back," Elliott said to E.T.

as they headed downstairs for dinner. After dinner the kids went to play in Elliott's room.

"I'm from Earth. Earth. Home," Elliott said to E.T. "Where are you from?"

E.T. pointed to the window. So Elliott opened the atlas to the picture of the solar system. E.T. found some balls of clay on Elliott's desk and placed the balls on the book. The balls slowly rose in the air. They watched in amazement until Elliott screamed and the balls dropped to the ground.

"What's happening?" asked Michael.

"I don't know. I just feel scared," Elliott said.

The kids went to check outside for any danger, and left E.T. alone with a pot of dying flowers that Gertie had brought for him earlier. Leafing through Gertie's coloring book, he saw a picture of beautiful flowers.

Seeing the drooping flowers next to him, E.T. concentrated on the pot. Suddenly the flowers bloomed back to life.

The next day E.T. had to stay in the house while Elliott went to school. Wandering through the kitchen, E.T. tried some food from the refrigerator. Then he played with some of Gertie's toys. Then he sat on the couch and turned the television on. A spaceship came on the television screen and E.T. made a moaning sound. It sounded like he was crying.

Meanwhile in science class, Elliott was learning how to dissect frogs, but he couldn't concentrate. He stared and stared at the frog in the jar on his desk. He felt bad for the frog, so he decided to set it free.

"Run for your lives!" shouted Elliott as he began to free every frog in the classroom.

At home E.T. watched a man kiss a woman on TV. Suddenly Elliott kissed a girl in his class. Strange things were happening.

Mary and Gertie came home before Elliott, but luckily Mary was too busy to notice E.T. Gertie watched television with E.T. She stood right in front of the screen and repeated the words she heard: "Basket. Bandit. Ball. B."

"B," said E.T.

"You can talk!" she exclaimed. "Good!"

"Be good," said E.T. Then he pointed to the telephone.

"You want to call somebody?" Gertie asked, confused. E.T. didn't answer.

"Look what he brought up all by himself," Gertie said when Elliott came home. Gertie had also put all of her dress-up clothes on E.T. Elliott groaned when he saw him. She ignored Elliott's groan and showed him a pile of household items that E.T. had dragged to Elliott's room. "What does he need all this stuff for? Oh, and he can talk now. I taught him how."

Elliott didn't believe her. "Can you say your name, E.T.?" he said.

"E.T.," E.T. repeated.

Elliott's eyes widened in surprise.

Just then E.T. waddled to the window and pointed outside. "E.T. home. Phone."

"E.T. phone home?" he asked.

"E.T. phone home," he agreed excitedly as Michael walked in the room.

Elliott knew exactly what he had to do. He had to help E.T. call his home.

"You know, Elliott, he doesn't look too good lately," Michael said while they looked in the garage for things to help E.T. make his communicator.

"Don't say that," snapped Elliott. "We're fine."

"What do you mean 'we'?"

"I mean he's fine," Elliott answered. He couldn't explain why he felt the things E.T. felt. He just knew he felt them. What he didn't know about was the van full of men spying on them parked outside his house.

Back in his room Elliott reached into the supply box from the garage and cut his finger on something sharp.

"Ouch!" Elliott shouted.

"Ouch!" E.T. repeated.

Just then E.T. extended his crooked finger toward Elliott. The tip glowed a yellowish green, and with a quick wave of his shining finger, he healed Elliott's cut!

The next day was Halloween. E.T. finished the communicator and they made a plan to take him to the forest so he could phone home.

"You all look so great!" squealed Mary as she ran to get her camera. Everyone was dressed up in Halloween costumes. Mary thought it was Gertie dressed as a ghost, but Gertie had gone ahead, and E.T. had taken her place under the white sheet. "Be back one hour after sundown," Michael whispered to Elliott when they got outside.

Elliott rode his bike as fast as he could, while E.T. sat tucked into the front basket. When it got too bumpy, E.T. rose the bike into the air. Suddenly they flew over the trees and past the moon.

"Wow!" shouted Elliott. "We're flying!"

When they landed safely on the ground, E.T. set up his communicator.

"It's working!" shouted Elliott as the wind set the machine in motion. E.T. stared up sadly into the sky. "Don't worry. They'll come soon," Elliott said.

Elliott awoke the next morning in the forest alone. E.T. was nowhere in sight.

"Where were you?" said Mary, hugging him tightly when he walked through the door. "Don't you ever do that again."

Michael went out to search for E.T. and found him lying sick in a creek. When he got home, Elliott was also very sick. Michael knew he had to tell his mom their secret. He brought her to Elliott and E.T. in the bathroom.

"We're sick," Elliott said weakly. "I think we're dying."

Mary scooped up Elliott and ran to the front door, but the men spying on them had surrounded the entire house. Doctors and scientists in space suits put Elliott and E.T. on examining tables.

"You can't do this," shouted Elliott. "He came to me! E.T!"

"Elliott," E.T. called back. The doctors were amazed to hear the alien speak.

However, the more strength Elliott gained, the worse E.T. got. And then he stopped breathing. "Look what they've done to you!" Elliott cried out.

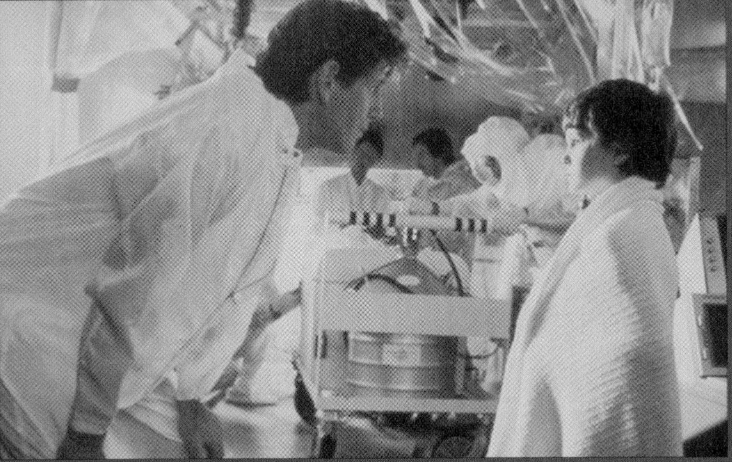

Elliott began to walk away toward the wilting flowerpot Gertie had left near E.T. All of a sudden, the flowers came back to life! Elliott turned back toward E.T. and saw a red glow coming from his heart.

"E.T. phone home!" shouted E.T. He was alive!

"Does this mean they're coming?" Elliott asked him excitedly.

"Yes! E.T. phone home! E.T. phone home!"

Overjoyed, Elliott found Michael and made a plan to take E.T. to his spaceship.

Michael sneaked into the driver's seat of the van that the doctors had put E.T. in, and Elliott jumped in the back. Michael's friends followed on their bikes. They tried to escape the cars that were now following them. But soon the men had them cornered, so Michael and Elliott got out of the van and jumped onto their bikes and put E.T. in the basket again. Then E.T. lifted all the bikes in the air and everyone flew across the sky.

Just after they landed in the forest, a beam of light shone from the sky. E.T. looked up and called out simply, "Home."

The spaceship landed in the tall grass. Everyone watched, even Mary and Gertie who had also come. E.T. said good-bye to Gertie and Michael. Then he stepped closer to Elliott.